ALL IN THE WOODLAND EARLY

ALL IN THE WOODLAND EARLY
≥ An ABC Book ≤

By Jane Yolen   Illustrations by Jane Breskin Zalben

Music and Lyrics by the author

COLLINS

The artist, author and publishers wish to express their
special thanks to the Children's Librarians of the
Port Washington Public Library for their assistance
with the research for this book.

Library of Congress Cataloging in Publication Data
Yolen, Jane   All in the woodland early.   Summary:
A woodland hunt reveals animals from A to Z. Includes musical score.
[1. Alphabet.   2. Animals—Fiction.   3. Stories to rhyme]
I. Zalben, Jane Breskin.   II. Title.   PZ8.3.Y76Al   [E]   79-10843
ISBN 0-529-05508-2   /   ISBN 0-529-05509-0 lib. bdg.

To Alexander,
who is learning his ABC's

One morning, one morning, one morning in May,
    All in the woodland early,
I saw a young fellow a-making his way
    All in the woodland early.
And where are you going so early today?
"I'm going a-hunting," was all he would say,
    All in the woodland early.

I saw an ANT running,
I saw a black BEAR,
  All in the woodland early;

A

B

I saw a small CHIPMUNK,
I saw a brown DEER,
    All in the woodland early.

I saw a swift EAGLE,
A FOX in his lair,
I saw a fine GOOSE,
And I saw a young HARE,
   All in the woodland early.
And where are you going this morning in May?
"We're going a-hunting," was all they would say.

I saw a green INCHWORM
Upon a green tree,
    All in the woodland early;
A JAY on one limb
Started screaming at me,
    All in the woodland early.

I saw a KINGSNAKE
And a LYNX running fast,
A MOUSE and a MINK
Blinked as *they* hurried past,
    All in the woodland early.

And where are you going this morning in May?
"We're going a-hunting," was all they would say.

I saw a shy NEWT;
An OPOSSUM played dead,
All in the woodland early.

A PHEASANT and PARTRIDGE
Flew right past my head,
   All in the woodland early.

I heard a loud QUAIL
As he took to his wings,
I saw a young RACCOON
And counted his rings,
    All in the woodland early.

And where are you going this morning in May?
"We're going a-hunting," was all they would say.

I saw a striped SKUNK
And I saw a small SHREW,
　　All in the woodland early;
A TURKEY came trotting
Right into my view,
　　All in the woodland early.

I saw an URBANUS,

A velvety VOLE,

And a very young WOODCHUCK
Just leaving his hole,
  All in the woodland early.

And where are you going this morning in May?
"We're going a-hunting," was all they would say.

I saw XYLEBORUS
Upon a tall tree,
  All in the woodland early;

I heard YELLOW JACKET
A-buzzing near me,
  All in the woodland early.

And last of all, ZEMMI,
Who's usually slow,
Ran out and went with them—
But where did they go,
    All in the woodland early?

"Hunting, we're hunting," I heard them all say.
How *can* you go hunting on such a fine day?

"We're hunting for *friends!* Won't you come out and play,
    All in the woodland early?"

All In The Woodland Early

J. Yolen

Music and Lyrics by
Jane Yolen

(To be sung)

One morning, one morning, one morning in May,
   All in the woodland early,
I saw a young fellow a-making his way
   All in the woodland early.
And where are you going so early today?
"I'm going a-hunting," was all he would say,
   All in the woodland early.

(To be sung)

I saw an ANT running,
I saw a black BEAR,
   All in the woodland early;
I saw a small CHIPMUNK,
I saw a brown DEER,
   All in the woodland early.
I saw a swift EAGLE,
A FOX in his lair,
I saw a fine GOOSE,
And I saw a young HARE,
   All in the woodland early.

   (To be spoken, rhythmically)
   And where are you going this morning in May?
   "We're going a-hunting," was all they would say.

(To be sung)

I saw a green INCHWORM
Upon a green tree,
   All in the woodland early;
A JAY on one limb
Started screaming at me,
   All in the woodland early.
I saw a KINGSNAKE
And a LYNX running fast,
A MOUSE and a MINK
Blinked as *they* hurried past,
   All in the woodland early.

   (To be spoken)
   And where are you going this morning in May?
   "We're going a-hunting," was all they would say.

(To be sung)

I saw a shy NEWT,
An OPOSSUM played dead,
   All in the woodland early.
A PHEASANT and PARTRIDGE
Flew right past my head,
   All in the woodland early.
I heard a loud QUAIL
As he took to his wings,
I saw a young RACCOON
And counted his rings,
   All in the woodland early.

   (To be spoken)
   And where are you going this morning in May?
   "We're going a-hunting," was all they would say.

(To be sung)

I saw a striped SKUNK
And I saw a small SHREW,
   All in the woodland early;
A TURKEY came trotting
Right into my view,
   All in the woodland early.
I saw an URBANUS,
A velvety VOLE,
And a very young WOODCHUCK
Just leaving his hole,
   All in the woodland early.

   (To be spoken)
   And where are you going this morning in May?
   "We're going a-hunting," was all they would say.

(To be sung)

I saw XYLEBORUS
Upon a tall tree,
   All in the woodland early;
I heard YELLOW JACKET
A-buzzing near me,
   All in the woodland early.
And last of all, ZEMMI,
Who's usually slow,
Ran out and went with them—
But where did they go,
   All in the woodland early?

(To be spoken)

"Hunting, we're hunting," I heard them all say.
How *can* you go hunting on such a fine day?
"We're hunting for *friends!* Won't you come out and play,
   All in the woodland early?"

The art for this book was prepared with a 000 brush,
watercolor and pencil on Opaline Parchment.
The type face is Goudy Old Style set by Concept Typographic Services.
Printed by Federated Lithographers-Printers Inc.
Bound by The Book Press.